In the S of the Volcano

By Caryn Jenner

LONDON, NEW YORK, MUNICH, MELBOURNE, AND DELHI

DK LONDON
Series Editor Deborah Lock
US Senior Editor Shannon Beatty
Assistant Editor Katy Lennon
Project Art Editor Ann Cannings
Producers, Pre-production
Francesca Wardell, Vikki Nousiainen

DK DELHI
Editor Pomona Zaheer
Assistant Art Editor Yamini Panwar
DTP Designers Anita Yadav, Nityanand Kumar
Picture Researcher Aditya Katyal
Deputy Managing Editor Soma B. Chowdhury

Reading Consultant
Linda Gambrell, Ph.D.

First American Edition, 2014

Published in the United States by
DK Publishing
345 Hudson Street, 4th Floor
New York, New York 10014

14 15 16 17 18 10 9 8 7 6 5 4 3 2 1
001—256561—July/2014
Copyright © 2014 Dorling Kindersley Limited

Published in Great Britain by Dorling Kindersley Limited.

A catalog record for this book is available from the Library of Congress.

ISBN: 978-1-4654-1979-8 (pb)
ISBN: 978-1-4654-1980-4 (plc)

DK books are available at special discounts when purchased in bulk for sales promotions, premiums, fund-raising, or
educational use. For details, contact: DK Publishing Special Markets, 345 Hudson Street, 4th Floor, New York, New York
10014 or SpecialSales@dk.com.

Printed and bound in China by South China Printing Company.

The publisher would like to thank the following for their kind permission
to reproduce their photographs:
(Key: a-above; b-below/bottom; c-center; f-far; l-left; r-right; t-top)
1 Fotolia: Beboy. **4–5 SuperStock:** Tips Images (b). **6–7 Dorling Kindersley:** Donks Models – Modelmaker (Volcano Model).
16–17 Alamy Images: Roberto Fumagalli (b). **22 Dorling Kindersley:** Rough Guides (cr). **23 Corbis:** Eurasia Press/Steven Vidler (tl);
John Heseltine (cra). **Dorling Kindersley:** Rough Guides (b). **24 Corbis:** Christie's Images (crb); Franz Richard Unterberger (cra).
Getty Images: De Agostini (bc). **25 Corbis:** Alinari Archives (ca); Bettmann (br). **Getty Images:** (bl). **27 Getty Images:** National
Geographic/Carsten Peter (b). **29 Corbis:** Blend Images/Chris Clor (t). **32 Dreamstime.com:** Parys (b). **34–35 Corbis:** Michael S.
Yamashita. **36–37 Corbis:** Gary Braasch. **38 Dorling Kindersley:** Atlantic Digital (cla). **42–43 Corbis:** Michael S. Lewis (b).
44 Corbis: Bettmann (ca); (br). **44–45 Dreamstime.com:** Jakub Krechowicz (Old Book Background). **45 Corbis:** Bettmann (t, b).
46 Dorling Kindersley: The Natural History Museum (b). **50 Dreamstime.com:** Shawn Hempel (Frame). **51 Dreamstime.com:** Shawn
Hempel. **52–53 Science Photo Library:** Planetary Visions Ltd (t). **52 Alamy Images:** Tom Pfeiffer (br). **53 Alamy Images:** Ashley
Cooper (br). **Corbis:** Reuters/Sigit Pamungkas (cl). **64 Alamy Images:** Leigh Prather (Page). **68–69 Dreamstime.com:** Christoph Weihs
(Paper). **70 Corbis:** Douglas Peebles (tr). **71 Corbis:** Gary Braasch (tr). **75 Alamy Images:** LatitudeStock. **77 Alamy Images:** Visions of
America, LLC (b). **78 Corbis:** zweimalig GbR. **80–81 Dreamstime.com:** Joshua Rainey (b). **82 Dorling Kindersley:** The Natural History
Museum (cra, cla, crb). **83 Dorling Kindersley:** The Natural History Museum (cr, clb, crb). **84 Corbis:** Ocean (clb); Vince Streano (cra).
85 Corbis: Douglas Kirkland (cr). **Getty Images:** John T. Barr (tl); National Geographic (b). **90 Corbis:** Reuters/STRINGER/ITALY
(b). **92 Corbis:** Stocktrek Images. **96–97 Dorling Kindersley:** Mark Longworth. **100 Alamy Images:** Pavel Borisov (cra); Stocktrek
Images, Inc. (cl). **101 Alamy Images:** Classic Image (tl); INTERFOTO (cra). **Corbis:** Sygma/Jacques Langevin (clb).
102 Corbis: Robert Harding World Imagery/Annie Owen. **103 Corbis:** Ocean. **105 Corbis:** Stocktrek Images/Richard Roscoe.
106 Corbis: Alberto Garcia. **112–113 Dorling Kindersley:** Rough Guides (b). **114 Dreamstime.com:** Martin Applegate (bl).
115 Corbis: Ocean (tr). **116–117 Corbis:** Douglas Peebles. **123 Corbis:** Douglas Peebles (b).
Jacket images: Front: 123RF.com: ammit; **Back: Corbis:** Alberto Garcia (t); **Spine: Corbis:** Gary Braasch (b).

All other images © Dorling Kindersley
For further information see: www.dkimages.com

Discover more at
www.dk.com

Contents

4 The Location

6 Volcano Fact File 1

8 Know Your Evacuation Plan

10 **Chapter 1** Lurking in the Shadow

26 **Chapter 2** Looming in the Shadow

40 **Chapter 3** Rumbling in the Shadow

56 **Chapter 4** The Awakening Shadow

72 **Chapter 5** Bursting Out of the Shadow

88 **Chapter 6** The Menacing Shadow

104 **Chapter 7** Escaping the Shadow

118 Epilogue

122 In the Shadow of the Volcano Quiz

124 Glossary

126 Index

127 About the Author and Consultant

The Location

Mount Vesuvius, an active volcano, overlooks the Bay of Naples in Italy. At 4,190 ft (1,277 m) above sea level, the summit can be reached by a road and then a spiral walkway. Since 1845, an observation center has been sited on the west slope.

ITALY

The area around Mt. Vesuvius is a national park. On the lower slopes, fruits, including grapes, are grown in the rich mineral lava soil. This gives them a special taste.

VENICE

FLORENCE

ITALY

ROME

NAPLES
AND
MT. VESUVIUS

SARDINIA

SICILY

Mt. Vesuvius is 5.6 miles (9 km) east of the large town of Naples. Villages are on the slopes and at the foot of the mountain.

CANTIERI del MEDITERRANEO

The Earth is separated into four layers: the inner core, outer core, mantle, and crust. The inner and outer cores together form a large metal ball that is 4,350 miles (7,000 km) across. Surrounding this is a mass of rock called the mantle, which is filled with magma—an iron-rich metal that explodes up through the crust to the Earth's surface when there is a volcanic eruption.

CLASSES OF VOLCANOES

Extinct volcano: a volcano that is never likely to erupt again.

Dormant volcano: a volcano that is not currently erupting but might erupt again.

Active volcano: a volcano that erupts frequently.

Solid crust

Mantle

This diagram shows the parts of a volcano.

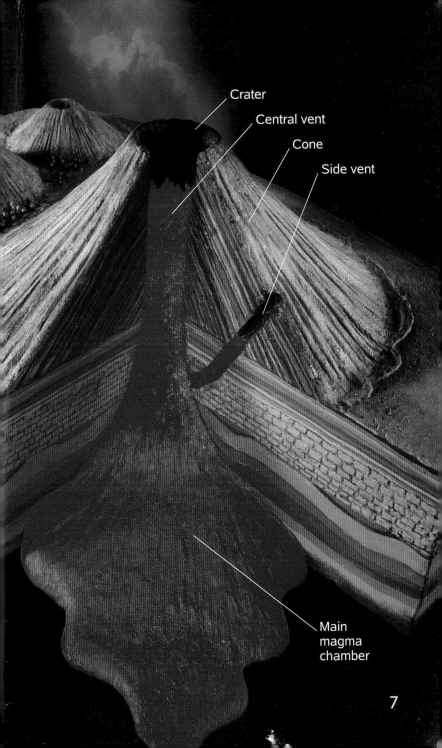

Crater

Central vent

Cone

Side vent

Main
magma
chamber

Know Your

Be prepared for a volcanic eruption

ALWAYS REMEMBER
During an eruption

▲ Listen to the local radio and evacuate only if told to do so by evacuation authorities.

▲ Avoid areas that are downwind of a volcano, and also river valleys that are downstream. This is often where debris will fall.

▲ When you are told to leave the house, change into a long-sleeved shirt and long pants. Use goggles and a dust mask. (If you don't have a dust mask, hold a damp cloth over your face.)

▲ If you are told to stay inside, close all windows and doors, and block chimneys and other vents to prevent ash from coming into your house.

▲ If you get caught outside during a rockfall and can't find shelter, roll into a ball to protect your head.

Evacuation Plan

After an eruption

▲ When leaving the house, be aware that it still may not be safe. Make sure you continue to wear long clothing, goggles, and a dust mask. It is not completely safe until authorities have told you so.

▲ Ash is surprisingly heavy. If there is a lot on the roof of your house, it will need to be cleared to stop the roof from caving in. Ensure that you are well protected while you are helping to clear this.

WATCH FOR THESE WARNING SIGNS IN YOUR NEIGHBORHOOD

NORMAL
No signs that volcano is about to erupt.

ADVISORY
Volcano is more active and could erupt very soon.

WATCH
Volcano is restless. An eruption may happen.

WARNING
Volcano is erupting. Evacuate the area!

CHAPTER 1
Lurking in the Shadow

"Carlo!" Rosa Carelli called down the hallway to her son. "Hurry or you'll be late for school."

"Can't I skip school and go to work with you instead, Mama?"

Twelve-year-old Carlo appeared in the hallway, his white school shirt hanging out of his pants and his red-and-black striped school tie in his hand.

"I could help you predict when Vesuvius is going to explode," he said.

NORMAL

WATCH

"Volcanoes erupt, Carlo. They don't explode," said Rosa. "Haven't I taught you anything?"

"But it's like an explosion," Carlo insisted. "So can I go with you? Please, Mama. *Per favore*?"

"No, Carlo." Rosa shook her head in frustration. "I need to investigate near the crater today, right at the top of Vesuvius. It could be dangerous."

"So why are you going if it's so dangerous?" asked Carlo.

"Because I'm a volcanologist. It's my job. You know that," Rosa replied. "But don't worry. I'll be wearing protective gear and I'll be very careful. Now come and have breakfast before you go to school."

With a disappointed sigh, Carlo disappeared back to his bedroom. Rosa put the coffeepot on the table, followed by the rolls and butter.

ADVISORY WARNING

She leaned out to open the shutters that covered the windows on either side of the room. The bright morning sun lit up the apartment. Rosa never tired of the view from here. The village of Montevista sat about two-thirds down the mountain of Vesuvius. The back window looked out on to the upper slopes of the mountain, while the front window overlooked the piazza. Today, the piazza was abuzz with activity as villagers prepared colorful stalls for tomorrow's festival. The Bay of Naples sparkled in the distance under the blue sky. On all sides of the mountain, more pretty villages dotted the landscape between lush fields and vineyards.

Vesuvius was certainly beautiful, thought Rosa. But deep inside the mountain, she knew there was danger lurking. Vesuvius was a volcano that was preparing to erupt. The only question was when.

NORMAL　　　　　　　**WATCH**

ADVISORY

WARNING

Carlo entered the kitchen, wearing his school uniform properly, ready for school.

"Mayor Fabiano doesn't think the volcano will be dangerous," he pointed out.

"Mayor Fabiano doesn't want anything to get in the way of tomorrow's village festival," Rosa replied, as she poured the hot coffee into her mug. "To him the Montevista Festival is the most important thing in the world. He doesn't realize that all of these small earthquakes we've been having lately are signs, leading up to a big volcanic eruption."

"Luigi's parents said that many other towns and villages on Vesuvius are getting ready to evacuate," said Carlo.

He took a big bite of a roll. Until this recent scare, he and his friend, Luigi, had often collected rocks near the crater at the top of the mountain. They liked meeting the tourists who climbed up the steep path that led to the crater, but now no one was allowed to go anywhere near it—except volcanologists like his mother.

Montevista
festival
lots of fun for everyone
Saturday July 14 at 2:00 PM
Village piazza

"The mayor should be prepared to put the evacuation plan into action," Rosa told him. "We don't know *exactly* when the volcano will erupt, but the data points to sooner rather than later. I say it's better to be safe than sorry, but our esteemed Mayor Fabiano says don't worry, everything is fine, *bene*. Never mind that

NORMAL   **WATCH**

the hot magma in the Earth is getting ready to boil over."

Carlo laughed. "He thinks because he is the mayor, he can tell the mighty Vesuvius when to erupt and when not to erupt."

Rosa couldn't help grinning at her son's funny remark.

"Not even the mayor can do that!"

"Doesn't he know what happened at Pompeii and Herculaneum?" asked Carlo. "Our teacher said that when Vesuvius erupted in ancient Roman times, the people didn't know they were in danger, so they stayed and watched. And then the ash and lava killed them."

"That's right," said Rosa, as she poured some more coffee. "After the eruption, there was a pyroclastic flow."

But this is the 21st century, not ancient Roman times, she thought. Her team at the Vesuvius Observation Center had the technology to predict when a volcano would erupt, and the towns and villages all had facilities to evacuate the people when the time came. If only Mayor Fabiano would take the warnings seriously.

"Nature will take its course, festival or no festival. The sizzling mixture of hot ash, rocks, and gases will erupt when it's ready," Rosa told Carlo.

Suddenly, the floor started shaking, and the lampshade over the table swayed. Quickly, Rosa got up and grabbed her son by the hand, pulling him toward the doorway. A sturdy doorway was the safest place to be during an earthquake—and there had already been dozens of small earthquakes this week. Nothing to cause serious damage or injury, but they were becoming stronger and more frequent.

Rosa knew that these mild earthquakes were an indication of a much larger shift occurring beneath the Earth. She held her son tight as the Earth rumbled and shook. Rosa flinched as she heard a crash from the kitchen. Then the Earth stopped moving and all was quiet.

"Okay, Carlo?" she asked him.

ADVISORY   WARNING

"Yeah, I'm fine," he said, grinning at his mother. "What's another earthquake? No big deal. How do you think this earthquake measured on the Richter scale? Stronger than yesterday's?"

"Definitely," said Rosa. "Let's wait here a moment longer in case there are aftershocks."

When Rosa and Carlo finally returned to the kitchen, they saw that the earthquake had caused the coffeepot to roll off the kitchen table, along with the rolls. Previous earthquakes had only caused a few things to rattle a bit. Vesuvius was getting closer and closer to erupting.

"Hey, who knows? Maybe Vesuvius will erupt today and school will be canceled," joked Carlo.

"It's not funny, Carlo," said Rosa, as she cleaned up the mess.

NORMAL   WATCH

She was tempted to keep him home from school today, just in case, and then they could be ready to evacuate at a moment's notice. But no, that would be overreacting. Even with all of their high-tech equipment, she and her team at the Observation Center couldn't predict the eruption that precisely. They didn't know yet whether the volcano would erupt today or next week or even next month.

Carlo will be fine, she told herself, and tomorrow's Montevista Festival will be wonderful as usual.

?

How did Rosa know this earthquake was stronger than the previous ones?

ADVISORY   WARNING

Tour starts here ➔

TOUR OF POMPEII

Tour introduction

Welcome, everybody, to our guided tour of the ancient Roman town, Pompeii. As we pass through the town, you will see the effects of the volcanic eruption of Mount Vesuvius in 79 CE. The eruption covered the town in a blanket of molten rock and ash and killed an estimated 16,000 people. The ash has preserved parts of this town for hundreds of years, ready for us to learn about its history today.

Eyewitness account

Pliny the Younger was a Roman author who witnessed the eruption of Vesuvius in 79 CE. Some of his letters about the event still exist today. Here he explains what the cloud of volcanic ash looked like:

"I can best describe its shape by likening it to a pine tree. It rose into the sky on a very long 'trunk' from which spread some 'branches.'"

He continues:

"broad sheets of flame were lighting up many parts of Vesuvius; their light and brightness were the more vivid for the darkness of the night... and then came a smell of sulfur, announcing the flames."

Volcanic ash and pumice stone buried the people of Pompeii leaving almost no survivors. Over the years, their bodies rotted away leaving only skeletons and air pockets where their bodies once were. Archeologists filled these air pockets with plaster to make casts of the ash-covered bodies.

❶ If you look to your right you will see the House of the Vettii, where two brothers who were wealthy merchants lived. We know this because the volcanic ash has preserved all of their expensive mosaics and artwork.

❷ This is the Macellum, a marketplace where people of Pompeii would go to buy fruits and vegetables.

❸ Up ahead is the amphitheater, where people used to go to watch gladiators fight.

Mount Vesuvius Eruptions

The eruption of 79 CE was one of the most famous, but Mt. Vesuvius has been continually active, causing great disruption. However, there has been no eruption since 1944, so anyone living in its shadow today is on constant alert.

1694 Another eruption had lava flowing from the crater.

1794 Torre del Greco was destroyed.

1600   **1700**

1631 On December 16, the lava claimed 600 victims, but Naples was saved.

1767 The lava reached San Giorgio a Cremano and approached Naples.

Timeline
1600–Present Day

1906 After another eruption, the crater widened by 985 ft (300 m).

1933 A series of shocks showed that the volcano was active once again. Lava appeared on June 3.

1800

1900

1880 The funicular opened to the public.

1944 After a final violent explosion, the trail of smoke disappeared.

CHAPTER 2
Looming in the Shadow

Rosa climbed up the slope, past the red *Danger Zone* signs, toward the crater at the top of Mt. Vesuvius. It was hard work in the bulky heatproof suit. Marco, her colleague from the Observation Center, was behind her. Rosa thought they must look like astronauts exploring a hostile planet.

"What's that dreadful odor?" asked Marco. "It smells like rotten eggs."

Rosa sniffed. Even through the heavy helmet, the smell was unmistakeable.

NORMAL   WATCH

"It's the sulfur from the volcano. The smell is a lot stronger than it has been and the tremors from that earthquake earlier were a lot stronger than the last one too."

"So that means..." said Marco, leaving his words hanging.

Rosa nodded. "Vesuvius is definitely getting ready to erupt, perhaps even sooner than we thought. Come on, let's take the readings and collect some rock samples to take back to the lab. Then we'll program VEX and get out of here."

ADVISORY   WARNING

Quickly, they got to work. Rosa called out the gas level readings and Marco sent the data back to the Observation Center on the computer. As Rosa had suspected, the sulfur levels had risen sharply even since yesterday. She knew that sulfur dioxide was one of the main gases found in magma, the hot rock that bubbled up inside volcanoes. A high reading meant that the magma was getting nearer to the surface.

Next, Rosa and Marco used an electronic thermometer to check the temperature of the rocks at specific locations around the perimeter of the crater. The rocks were all much hotter than yesterday's readings. Then they checked readings on the tiltmeters that were dotted around the crater area. The tiltmeters measured any changes in the slope of the ground.

"Look, Marco," said Rosa. "These tiltmeter readings are quite different than yesterday, especially in this spot here."

"That means the magma is pushing up from under the surface, doesn't it?" he asked.

"It certainly does," Rosa replied. "Come on, I think it's time to get VEX ready. It's getting too dangerous here for us."

VEX was short for Volcanic Explorer, a robotic vehicle that could collect and transmit data and video footage back to the Observation Center. It was designed to withstand the violent blast of a volcanic eruption, as well as the intense heat and poisonous gases that would be emitted.

Quickly, they retrieved VEX from the back of the 4x4 and programmed it. Rosa watched VEX set off up to the crater, its long tracks moving slowly but surely.

NORMAL   WATCH

She sighed. She had done what she could up here. It was up to VEX now.

Rosa thought about Carlo at school in Montevista. What if the volcano erupted and he couldn't escape? She turned around to look back down the mountain toward the village. She was surprised to see a man climbing up the slope toward them. He wore ordinary street clothes instead of protective gear and he was filming with a video camera.

ADVISORY   WARNING

"Who on earth is that?" she asked Marco.

"No idea," came the puzzled reply. "But he must have walked right past the *Danger Zone* signs."

As the man climbed toward them, Rosa could see that he was huffing and puffing, and his shirt was stained with sweat. Silly man, she thought. He looked somehow familiar, but she didn't know why.

"Hey, isn't that Aldo Rizzo, the news reporter from the TV?" said Marco.

NORMAL   WATCH

Of course, thought Rosa, and he was here for a news story.

"I'm sorry, Mr. Rizzo, but you'll have to leave," Rosa called to him. "The public is not allowed up here. It's too dangerous."

Aldo kept climbing. "But I'm not just anyone. I'm a journalist," he panted. "I've got to go wherever there's news, and Vesuvius erupting is certainly big news."

"Mr. Rizzo, you haven't even got a heatproof suit on," said Rosa firmly.

"I'm sure I can get one," he replied. "I didn't realize it was going to be so hot up here." He held his nose with his free hand. "Or smelly. *Mamma mia!*"

Just then, Rosa's cell phone rang. She saw on the phone screen that it was the Observation Center calling.

"Marco, can you deal with Mr. Rizzo while I take this," she said.

It was the chief scientist at the Observation Center. As Rosa heard what he had to say, she felt herself go cold despite the intense heat at the top of Vesuvius.

Quickly, she hung up and turned to Marco, who was still trying to persuade Aldo to leave.

"The satellites have detected a bulge just west of the crater that wasn't there yesterday," Rosa reported.

NORMAL   WATCH

Marco looked at Rosa for a moment as if he wasn't sure he had heard her correctly. Then he started gathering up their equipment.

"Good thing we've already programmed VEX. We'd better get out of here!"

"A bulge? You mean a bump on the side of the mountain?" said Aldo. "What does that mean?"

"It means Vesuvius is about to erupt!" said Rosa. "Now, let's get off the mountain!"

Do You Want to Be a Volcanologist?

 Are you interested in volcanoes?

 Are you good at finding clues and solving mysteries?

Do you like the outdoors?

Do you like science?

 Are you good at using computers and gadgets?

Do you want to travel all over the world?

Job description

The Young Volcanologists Club is currently recruiting for a new volcanologist. The job will include **trips** to **other countries** to **study active** and **dormant volcanoes**. You will be expected to carry out **research** about **how** and **why volcanoes erupt** and use our **special equipment** to predict when they will erupt again. You must have **nerves of steel** because active volcanoes could **erupt at any moment**!

You will need

■ **HEAVY BOOTS** to protect your feet from the sharp, dried lava.

■ **SILVER HEAT-RESISTANT SUIT** to protect your body from the intense heat near an active volcano.

■ **GAS MASK** to protect you from the invisible gases that are emitted from volcanoes.

■ **HEATPROOF GLOVES** to enable you to handle hot, dangerous samples.

■ **CAMERAS** to record findings at the volcanic site.

■ **COSPEC** (correlation spectrometer) to measure volcanic gases.

■ **ROBOT** to help collect samples from areas that volcanologists can't reach.

Volcano Fact File 2

Crater around central vent

1 Fissure volcano
This is a plateau shape as lava flows from a long crack.

TYPES OF VOLCANOES

These are the six kinds of volcanoes. The first three are formed by runny lava flows, spreading quickly over a large area. Violent eruptions create the last three. Some volcanoes combine features of more than one type.

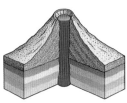

4 Ash-cinder volcano
This has slightly inward curving sides, formed by the pileup of ash, cinder, and lava.

DATA: **CRATERS**

Craters are dips at the top of a volcano.
These are blown out by an eruption
through the central vent. These may
be filled with rainwater to make a lake.
The largest craters are called calderas.
These can be up to 62 miles (100 km) wide.

❷ **Shield volcano**
This is low with gently
sloping sides, formed
by thin, runny lava
eruptions.

❸ **Dome volcano**
This is a circular
mound, formed
by quick-cooling
sticky lava.

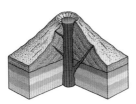

❺ **Composite volcano**
This has a tall, cone
shape with more than
one vent and alternating
layers of lava and ash.

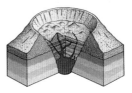

❻ **Caldera volcano**
This has a large
crater, formed by a
very violent eruption.

CHAPTER 3
Rumbling in
the Shadow

At last the bell rang. Carlo sighed with relief. The school day was finally over.

"Hey, Carlo!"

He turned around to see Luigi sauntering out of school behind him.

"How about going on a rock-collecting expedition?" Luigi asked.

"Where?" said Carlo. "We're not allowed anywhere near the crater. My mom says the volcano's going to erupt soon."

"Yeah, yeah," said Luigi. "We've been waiting for Vesuvius to erupt for months now. It's not going to happen any time soon. It's extinct."

"So how come we've been having all these earthquakes?" Carlo asked. "And how come the mountain smells so disgusting?"

Luigi laughed. "Anyway, I'm going rock-hunting up near Valetti's vineyard. Are you coming or not?"

"*Si, si*," Carlo answered. "Yes, I'm coming. Who knows? Maybe these earthquakes have uncovered some unusual specimens."

"Race you there!" called Luigi.

The two boys dashed out of the schoolyard, across the village piazza, and along a path that led to a dirt track. They followed the track past a field of tomatoes still green on the vine, and another field of zucchini just beginning to flower.

At last, they reached Valetti's vineyard, where plump purple grapes hung on the vines. However, Carlo and Luigi were more interested in the scrubland nearby. They put their schoolbags down and began picking up rocks to inspect them.

"What do you think this one is?" Luigi asked.

NORMAL   WATCH

Carlo glanced at it. "Basalt. I've got loads of it in the rock collection that my grandpa gave me. There are some really interesting specimens that he collected when he was a kid," he continued. "My grandpa tells stories about how he and his family escaped when Vesuvius erupted in 1944. Afterward, he found loads of amazing rocks."

Eruption at Vesuvius, 1944

Day 2: March 19,
Ash and lava bombs
thrown up to 500 ft
(150 m) into the air.
Lava flow continues.

Day 4: March 21,
Eruption column rises
1 mile (1.6 km) into
the air. Lava flow
decreases, but strong
lava fountains erupt.

Day 4: March 21, Already dispirited by war, residents of San Sebastiano evacuate as lava flows down the main street. US soldiers help with the evacuation.

Day 5: March 22, Eruption plume reaches height of 3–4 miles (5–6 km) above the crater rim.

"1944? Is that when the last eruption was? That's ages ago," said Luigi. "Vesuvius must be one of those sleeping volcanoes."

"You mean dormant," Carlo corrected him, "but when you're talking about geology, 1944 is like a nanosecond ago. It's hardly any time at all. Vesuvius is an active volcano."

The boys continued to inspect the rocks. Luigi filled his schoolbag with a variety of rocks that looked interesting. Meanwhile,

NORMAL   WATCH

Carlo found a rock that looked like granite with large quartz crystals embedded in it, and another that he thought might be gabbro. He would have to check it against his rock identification book at home.

"Luigi, do you feel something strange?" Carlo asked.

"What do you mean?" said his friend.

"I don't know exactly. Sort of like a weird vibration in your feet."

"Yeah, man; it's a funky rhythm," Luigi agreed, and wiggled his hips in a crazy dance.

Carlo laughed and decided to ignore the strange feeling.

Just then, he heard his cell phone ring tone. It was his mom calling.

"*Ciao*, Mama," he said into the phone.

"Carlo, meet me at home as soon as you can!"

"But Mama, Luigi and I are collecting rocks," he protested.

Carlo listened as his mother talked quickly.

"*Si*, Mama. Okay. You too. See you soon."

Carlo signed off. "I've got to go home," he told Luigi. "My mom says the volcano's going to blow soon. She says we need to drive down the mountain where we'll be safe."

Luigi burst out laughing. "Your mom takes her job too seriously. If Mayor Fabiano doesn't think we need to evacuate, that's good enough for me. Besides, I've been looking forward to the festival tomorrow!"

"Yeah, me too," said Carlo. "But what if my mom is right? I don't want to get roasted by hot lava or suffocated by ash."

He started down the path.

"Carlo, come here! *Vieni qui!*" called Luigi. "Look at this rock. I've never seen one like it before."

NORMAL   WATCH

Carlo couldn't resist. He turned around to look. "That's because it's not a rock; it's a grape!" he laughed.

"I've decided instead of a rock collection, I'll start a grape collection," said Luigi.

As Carlo watched, Luigi ran around the vineyard, picking up grapes from the ground. Then he started throwing them at Carlo, and Carlo just had to start throwing grapes back.

Suddenly, he stopped. He realized that the weird vibration in his feet was the Earth moving beneath him. It wasn't sharp jolts like this morning's earthquake. It was more of a steady rumble, as if something below the surface was about to boil over.

ADVISORY   WARNING

Volcanic Rock

All these rocks were once magma thrown out in a volcanic eruption and afterward cooled and crystallized. The formation of different types depends on how fast or slow they cool.

EXTRUSIVE ROCK:
formed by magma that has cooled on the crust's surface.

Basalt is mostly formed on ocean floors. It commonly contains lots of little holes formed by gas bubbles.

Obsidian has a glassy texture caused by the fast cooling of sticky hot lava.

INTRUSIVE ROCK:

formed from magma that has cooled under the surface of the Earth.

Granite is the most common intrusive rock and is recognizable by its mottled pink, white, gray, and black surface.

Gabbro is formed when molten magma is trapped beneath the Earth's surface and cools.

Pegmatite has large crystals due to a high amount of water in the magma when it cools.

The Big Buildup

Volcanologists are unable to predict exactly when a volcano will erupt, but they are able to provide eruption warnings. The clues are given in the data collected from their scientific equipment.

Gravimetry station
This equipment measures the magnetic pull (field of gravity) of the magma within a volcano. This measurement changes if the magma mass moves. These movements could trigger an eruption.

Landsat images
Visual images taken from a satellite help to identify changes in the landscape of an area. Infrared and thermal images can also show the buildup of heat on the ground.

satellite receiver

Global Positioning System (GPS)
This system of satellites records the position of the ground and will pick up on any changes. As magma rises, its pressure makes the surface tilt or bulge.

tripod

17.

Famous Volcanoes

Every day, at least one volcano is erupting somewhere on Earth. Some volcanoes have become infamous for one of their dramatic and devastating eruptions.

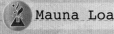 Mount St. Helens

 Mauna Loa

ATLANTIC OCEAN

PACIFIC OCEAN

The red triangles on this map mark the world's volcanoes. More than 75% of the active volcanoes are found in a string around the edge of the Pacific Ocean called the Ring of Fire. Around 90% of the world's earthquakes also strike in the Ring.

Name	Major eruption	Place
Mauna Loa	Continuous	Hawaii, USA
Mount Pinatubo	1991	Luzon, Philippines
Mount St. Helens	1980	Washington, USA
Tambora	1815	Sumbawa, Indonesia
Mount Vesuvius	79 CE	Pompeii, Italy

Mount Vesuvius

Mount Pinatubo

Tambora

INDIAN OCEAN

SOUTHERN OCEAN

CHAPTER 4
The Awakening Shadow

Rosa could feel the vibrations, too. She pictured the hot magma and gases moving around inside the volcano in what was known as a harmonic tremor—a sign that the eruption was getting closer and closer.

"Where is that boy?" Rosa said to herself, as she directed traffic around the village

NORMAL   WATCH

piazza. She now wore a fluorescent yellow safety vest and carried a megaphone to help keep order.

"No passing please," she called through the megaphone. "I know you're all in a hurry, but accidents won't help you get away quicker."

All around her, people were jumping into their cars, beeping their horns, and setting off down the road that led away from the volcano to safety.

"Marco!" Rosa called through the megaphone. He hurried over. "Have you seen my son anywhere?"

"No, I haven't," Marco replied, "but I'll keep an eye out for him."

Rosa sighed. "Thanks. If you do see him, tell him to come to the piazza. Tell him it's urgent! I must get him to safety."

"I'll tell him, Rosa," Marco promised.

ADVISORY   **WARNING**

"Here!" She gave him the keys to the 4x4. "Can you drive out to help evacuate people on the farms and in the outlying areas of the village? Take the megaphone, too."

"What about you?" asked Marco. "Won't you and Carlo need the 4x4 to evacuate?"

"We'll use my old Vespa scooter," she replied. "Now go!"

Rosa glanced down at her phone. No calls from Carlo.

BEEP! BEEP-BEEP! Car horns blared.

Everyone was in a hurry—and who could blame them? It was Rosa herself who had set the evacuation plan into action. She and Marco had shown Mayor Fabiano the data, but he refused to believe it.

"Just one more day," he had said. "Just wait until after the festival tomorrow."

Rosa didn't want to take that chance.

Evacuation Plan

Due to increased seismic activity in areas around Mt. Vesuvius, the Montevista Council is issuing an evacuation warning to all residents within a 12 mile (20 km) radius of the crater.

NO IMMEDIATE ACTION is required, but please listen to the local radio station and initiate the evacuation procedure if ordered to do so by your local council.

PLEASE MAKE THE FOLLOWING PREPARATIONS

Have the following items prepared:

- ☑ flashlight and extra batteries,
- ☑ first aid kit and essential medicines,
- ☑ emergency food and water,
- ☑ sturdy shoes,
- ☑ battery powered radio,
- ☑ dust mask and goggles.

When ordered to evacuate, do not panic. Make your way calmly and quickly down the mountain to one of the evacuation centers outside the exclusion zone.

ADVISORY

WARNING

So now everyone was leaving—everyone except Mayor Fabiano. She could see him on the piazza, in the midst of colorful stalls and festival banners, telling anyone who would listen that they should stay for tomorrow's festival, and then leave.

He made his way across the piazza toward her until his short, stout frame was right in front of her, blocking the cars. BEEP! BEEP! went the horns.

NORMAL   WATCH

The mayor twirled his gray moustache.

"For the first time in centuries, the Montevista Festival will not happen," he told her. "Thanks to you, there will be no one here to enjoy it tomorrow."

"At least the people will be safe from the volcano," Rosa replied.

"You don't know exactly when the volcano will erupt," said the mayor. "You can't predict it with absolute certainty."

ADVISORY   **WARNING**

"That's true," Rosa admitted, "but I've already shown you the scientific data that indicates Vesuvius will erupt very soon. Surely it's better to be safe than to risk lives for the sake of the festival."

He shook his head. "You're just causing everyone needless panic."

Rosa couldn't believe what she was hearing. "Mayor Fabiano, you are aware of what happened at the ancient Roman towns of Pompeii and Herculaneum? When Vesuvius erupted and killed many people? Well, I'm trying to prevent that happening again. Who would want that tragic fate if they've got a warning, a chance to escape?"

As she said this, Rosa thought again of Carlo. Where was he?

Just then, someone tapped her on the shoulder. Rosa spun around, hoping it was Carlo, but it was Aldo Rizzo.

"We meet again," he said.

"Mr. Rizzo, you should be headed down the mountain to safety like everyone else," Rosa told him.

"I'm staying here to film the volcano," said Aldo.

"*Bene!* Good!" The mayor slapped Aldo's back to congratulate him. "Stay and film the festival tomorrow, too. It'll be good publicity for the village."

Aldo grinned and held up his video camera. "Shall I interview you right now, Mayor Fabiano?"

"Fabulous! That will be very good publicity!"

The mayor twirled his gray moustache and cleared his throat. He glanced at Rosa.

"Crazy fools," Rosa muttered under her breath, as she went back to directing the traffic and looking out for Carlo.

Festival
Timetable

10:00 AM Opening Ceremony

12 noon Carnival Procession

2:00 PM Donkey Race

4:00 PM Wine Tasting

6:00 PM Folk Dancing

10:00 PM Fireworks

NORMAL   WATCH

At the same time, Rosa listened in on the interview. The mayor went on and on about how brilliant the Montevista Festival was going to be and how it was such an old tradition in the village. It was all true. Ordinarily, Rosa loved the colorful atmosphere and fun of the annual festival. However, the mayor neglected to mention an important issue affecting this year's event—the volcano was about to erupt!

Finally, Aldo asked, "And what about the volcano warnings, Mayor?"

"The great Mount Vesuvius is one of the main attractions of the area," the mayor replied. "Of course it has the potential to erupt at any time. It is a volcano after all, but we can't worry about every little thing. Here in Montevista, we believe in living life to the full. Come to the festival tomorrow and let us show you!"

Rosa couldn't believe what she was hearing, and interrupted, "Mayor, you are well aware that this volcano warning is not just a little worry. It's very serious!"

Suddenly, she realized that Aldo had turned his camera on her.

"I'm Rosa Carelli, a volcanologist with the Vesuvius Observatory," she said directly into the camera. "We're advising everyone to evacuate and go down the mountain to the safety zone. There is scientific evidence that an eruption is about to happen!"

"I saw a volcano erupting on vacation once in Hawaii," Aldo said into the camera. "The lava spurting out was a beautiful sight. Many tourists go to see the volcanoes there."

"However, we know that Vesuvius is a different kind of volcano," Rosa explained.

NORMAL

WATCH

"It's more like Mount St. Helens, which erupts with ash and lava bombs blasting out of the crater and spreading over the area."

BEEP! BEEP!

Rosa turned back to directing the traffic as the villagers heeded her advice and evacuated. Let Aldo and the mayor take their chances, but her scientific training—and her gut instinct—told her to join the cars and drive down the mountain to safety. But she wouldn't leave without Carlo. Where was he?

?

How would you feel if you were being evacuated from the village?

ADVISORY **WARNING**

GOVERNMENT NOTICE

🏃 EVACUATION WARNING!

Province of Naples

KEY

 Danger zone

Ash fallout exclusion zone

 Mudflow exclusion zone

 Safety zone

 Evacuation center

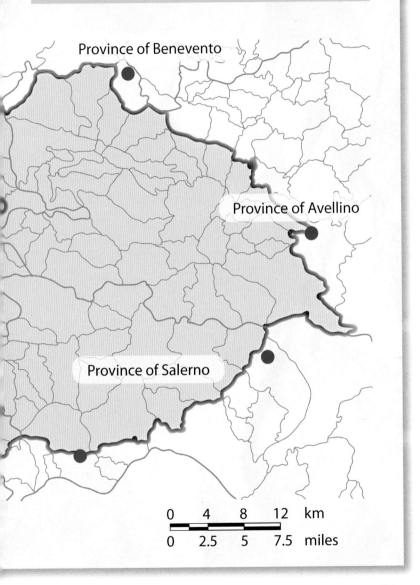

Which **volcanic activity** is your favorite? Two volcanologists discuss their favorite type of eruption and then let you decide.

Kilauea in Hawaii has erupted non-stop since 1983.

"The wonder of fountains of lava shot hundreds of feet into the air is an awesome sight. There is no hanging around waiting for action with these shield volcanoes since they are frequently active. Shooting jets and oozing lava overflow from the lava lake at its crater, creating fiery rivers of red-hot runny lava. These burning flows spread out across the landscape, slowly changing and shaping it. Everything burns in its path. We can watch with fascination the formations and folds of the lava as they cool. These eruptions are violent and beautiful, fascinating and stunning to watch and make the best photos."

Mount St. Helens erupted dramatically in 1980.

"The excitement of explosive eruptions is that they are unpredictable. After tens or even hundreds of years staying dormant, composite volcanoes then erupt with incredible and terrifying force. The volcanoes are like sleeping giants suddenly awoken. Pressure from hot gas and magma has built up underneath, blocked by a plug, unable to get out until this explosive moment of its sudden release. The blast sends clouds of hot gas, ash, lava bombs, and rocks billowing hundreds of feet into the air. These then rain down on the surrounding area. The effect is dramatic and particularly dangerous if the ash column collapses and a pyroclastic flow zooms down the sides. The landscape of the volcano has been changed until the next blast—who knows when?"

CHAPTER 5
Bursting Out of the Shadow

Carlo and Luigi trudged down the dirt track toward the village. They had to keep to the side, out of the way of the line of cars driving down the mountain.

"Strange, hardly anyone normally drives on here," said Carlo. The grape fight with Luigi had been fun, but now he was getting a strange feeling that something was wrong.

"Hey, are you still feeling that funky rhythm?" asked Luigi. "It's gotten faster, hasn't it?"

Carlo realized that it had. What if his mom was right about the volcano this time?

Just then, he heard his name being called.

"Carlo Carelli!"

Carlo looked around. Luigi pointed up ahead at the 4x4 sporting the logo of the Vesuvius Observation Center. Carlo expected to see his mom, but instead he saw Marco leaning out of the window, calling his name through a megaphone. The boys dodged the slow-moving line of traffic and ran over to see him.

The 4x4 was full of people clutching their belongings, including Luigi's parents.

"*Ciao!*" Luigi greeted them. "*Come va?* How's things?"

The people moved over to make space for Luigi as he climbed in.

"So," said Luigi, grinning at all the serious faces in the car, "where are we going?"

ADVISORY   **WARNING**

"Down the mountain to safety," said Marco. "The volcano's about to erupt! You hop in too, Carlo, and I'll give you a lift to the piazza. Your mom's there waiting for you. She's been going crazy with worry."

Carlo could see that it would take the 4x4 ages to get to the piazza in this traffic jam.

"I know a short cut by foot. It'll be quicker!" he told Marco.

He took off down the track as fast as he could, his legs pumping and his heart beating wildly. He felt like he was racing against the volcano. At last, he reached the path and then the piazza.

There was hardly anyone there, only Mayor Fabiano and a man with a video camera. They didn't look at all panicked.

"Have you seen my mom?" Carlo asked the mayor, gasping for breath.

ADVISORY

WARNING

"She's been worried about you, young man," said the mayor. "She does worry a lot, doesn't she?"

Carlo looked at the other man. "Hey, you're the reporter from the TV news, aren't you?" he asked in surprise.

The man grinned. "*Si, si*. That's me."

"Carlo, at last!" Rosa appeared from the alley next to their building on the edge of the piazza. She gave Carlo a warm hug and a kiss on each cheek. Normally he would have been embarrassed, but he could see the concern on his mother's face.

"I'm so sorry, Mama. Luigi and I, we—"

"There's no time now, Carlo. We need to hurry."

Rosa led Carlo to the alley where her old, rusty Vespa scooter was waiting. Rosa had attached the sidecar and filled it with a bundle of clothes and other things.

76

Carlo remembered how he used to ride in the sidecar when he was a little boy as his mom zoomed around on the scooter.

Rosa handed him a helmet and put one on herself. Then she climbed on to the scooter and gestured for Carlo to climb on behind her. She revved the engine and then they were off!

Carlo held tightly to his mom's waist as Rosa expertly leaned in and out of the curves in the road.

NORMAL   WATCH

He was grateful she hadn't lost her touch on the old scooter. He felt as if they were flying down the mountain road, winding round and round the legendary Mount Vesuvius.

Suddenly, the mountain shook with a fierce power! The scooter wobbled and Carlo held on to his mother, afraid they would topple off the mountain.

Quickly, Rosa maneuvered the scooter away from the edge of the road and they clambered off, huddling next to the upper slope. They clung on to each other as rocks and dirt fell down the slope on top of them, pinging off their helmets. Carlo closed his eyes, but still the world shook. He wondered if a crack was going to open up in the mountain and swallow them. This earthquake was by far the strongest yet.

ADVISORY

WARNING

When the shaking finally stopped, Carlo opened his eyes. He and his mom were alright, but the road was covered in rubble and he could see actual cracks in the mountain, with what looked like steam coming out. He smelled the distinct odor of rotten eggs.

Beneath her helmet, his mom's face was pale. "This is what happened at Mount St. Helens. First there was a violent earthquake and then the volcano erupted."

NORMAL

WATCH

Carlo's mind whirled. For some reason, what came into his head was an image of the nearly deserted piazza.

"What will happen to the mayor and that news reporter?" he asked. "They're still in Montevista."

Rosa made a quick decision. "We'll have to go back and get them. Let's go, Carlo!"

He climbed back onto the scooter behind his mother and together they raced over the rubble-strewn road back toward the village.

81

ADVISORY   **WARNING**

Volcanic Fragments

Lapilli are fragments 2–64 mm in size.

Ash consists of fine grains less than 2 mm in size.

Pele's hair refers to fine strands of lapilli shaped by strong winds.

Blocks or lava bombs are angular fragments 64 mm or bigger, made from andesite.

Spatter is formed of lapilli and block-size fragments that are airborne a short time, so are still liquid when they hit the ground.

Pumice is formed by bubbling, gas-filled liquid lava, cooling rapidly, leaving hollows. Pumice is light and can float.

Scoria is a heavy lava containing large bubbles.

Dust is fine powder of rock and mineral fragments.

Mount St. Helens Eruption, 1980

PRE-1980 SHAPE

A month before the May 1980 eruption, Mount St. Helens in Washington, USA, puffed out plumes of ash. We watched from a distance for days, wondering what else this awakening giant was planning.

THE COLUMN ROSE 15 MI (24 KM) HIGH

At 8:32 AM on May 18, 1980, an earthquake caused a huge landslide on the north face, taking the top off the mountain, triggering a powerful eruption. We watched speechless as a sideways blast of hot gas, ash, and rock came speeding down the mountainside, destroying everything in its path.

The hot rocks and gas melted the snow, and lahars (volcanic mudflows) surged down the mountain, ripping up trees and washing away bridges.

ASH-COVERED SNOW

Towns for many miles around were covered in a thick, dense ash-cloud that blackened the sky. Over 6 in. (15 cm) of ash fell.

TOWNS WERE EERILY SILENT.

Minor eruptions have occurred since, destroying and rebuilding the dome. Volcanologists continue to monitor the activity.

MEASURING GROWING CRACKS

Make Your Own Volcano

The chemical reactions that take place inside a volcano happen on a giant scale and cause huge eruptions. However, with a little bit of science know-how and a few household ingredients, you can recreate these on a smaller scale in your own kitchen.

You will need:

- vinegar in a bottle
- red food coloring
- baking soda
- small plastic bottle
- funnel
- sand

N.B. If you get any vinegar on your skin, wash it off with soap and water right away.

Instructions to follow

1 Mix the vinegar in a bottle with some red food coloring.

2 Using a funnel, half fill the small bottle with baking soda.

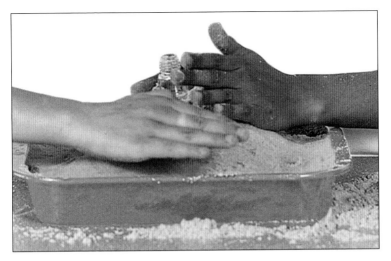

3 Put the small bottle of baking soda in the middle of a large dish or tray. Pile damp sand around it, making a volcano shape with the bottle in the middle.

4 Pour the vinegar mixture into the top of the soda bottle, step back, and watch your volcano erupt! The vinegar reacts with the chemicals in the soda.

CHAPTER 6
The Menacing Shadow

In Montevista, the festival stalls that had gaily lined the piazza now lay in heaps on the square. Rosa guessed they must have fallen over during the earthquake.

She looked at the yellow stucco building overlooking the piazza that was their home. Jagged cracks criss-crossed the walls and the shutters on the windows dangled dangerously over the sidewalk. Sadly, Rosa wondered what damage the earthquake had caused inside their beautiful apartment.

NORMAL   WATCH

She knew the earthquake was just for starters. Next was the volcanic eruption! What would happen then?

"Look, Mama!" Carlo pointed to a van sporting the same TV logo that was on the side of Aldo's video camera. A streetlamp had smashed through it. "That news reporter wouldn't have been able to leave now anyway. It's a good thing we came back."

Just then, they heard a shout.

"*Attenzione!* Over here! The mayor needs help."

Rosa and Carlo turned to see Aldo Rizzo getting to his feet from beneath a pile of debris on the piazza. They hurried over. Mayor Fabiano was lying under the festival banner, his face pale and his moustache drooping.

"Well, Rosa, you were right. There will be no festival after all." He winced in pain. "But it wasn't a volcano; it was an earthquake."

"I'm afraid the volcano is still going to erupt, Mayor, and soon. We've got to get you out of here quickly," Rosa replied.

"Would you help Aldo to move this heavy wooden pole, please? *Per favore*," said the mayor, grimacing. "It seems to have fallen on my foot."

Immediately, Rosa, Carlo, and Aldo grabbed hold of the pole.

"One, two, three," counted Rosa, and together, they heaved the pole off the mayor's foot and on to the ground.

The mayor sighed with relief. "That's much better. Thank you. *Grazie molte*."

Rosa ran to get the scooter and rode it on to the piazza. Meanwhile, the mayor put one arm around Aldo's shoulders and the other around Carlo's shoulders and hobbled over to meet her. Rosa noticed Carlo holding his nose with his free hand. She didn't blame him. The smell of sulfur was getting so strong now, it nearly made her choke. They had to get away before the volcano erupted!

Rosa threw the bundle of belongings out of the sidecar. "Mayor, you and Carlo get in here. Quickly now! You'll fit if you budge up. Aldo, you get on the back of the seat."

No one dared to object. They all climbed on without a word and a moment later, the scooter was headed back down the mountain.

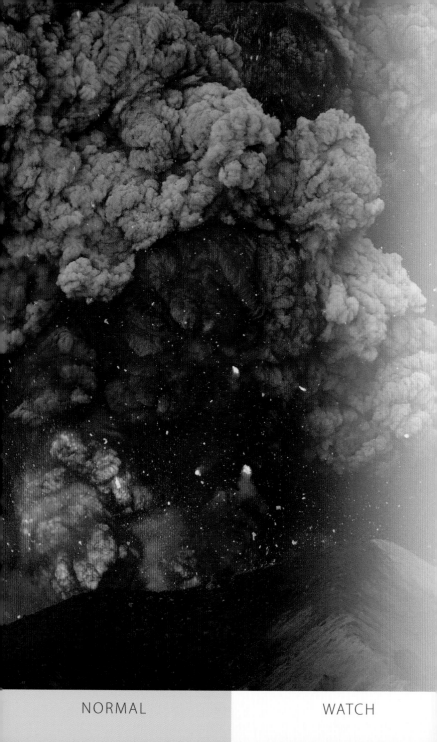

NORMAL   WATCH

Now that Rosa's little scooter was laden with four people, she found it even more difficult to maneuver over and around the rubble. She managed though, riding quickly but carefully. Soon they would all be safe. As they rode farther and farther down the mountain, Rosa allowed herself a sigh of relief.

It was then that Vesuvius erupted with a boom that echoed over the landscape!

The volcano shook and Rosa lost control of the scooter. Everyone held their breath as the scooter flew into the air and then landed back on the road with a bump. Rosa struggled to regain control. Part of her was desperate to see Vesuvius erupting—after all, she had spent years studying volcanoes—but she knew she had to keep her wits about her and her eyes firmly on the road.

93

ADVISORY   **WARNING**

Aldo clung on, terrified. In the sidecar, the mayor had shut his eyes in fear. It was Carlo who turned around to see a giant gray cloud of ash billowing up into the sky from the crater of Vesuvius. It covered the Sun and the blue sky above the mountain. The ash cloud seemed to crackle, and then bright bolts of lightning flashed across the sky, one after the other in a dazzling display.

Rosa sped ahead as fast as she possibly could with herself and three passengers weighing down the scooter. They had only just survived the eruption by the skin of their teeth. If they had left Montevista a few minutes later, they would have been caught in the eruption. However, now they were nearing the foot of the mountain, and the ground was leveling off. Only a little farther and they would reach the end of the exclusion zone, where they would be safe.

NORMAL   WATCH

But Rosa was well aware that they were on the west side of the mountain where the bulge had been spotted, and she knew that there was a danger of a pyroclastic flow. If she was right, then they didn't have much time...

?
Why is Rosa speeding as fast as she can?

ADVISORY   **WARNING**

Volcano Fact File 3

DATA: **ERUPTIONS!**

The intensity of a volcanic eruption depends on how much pressure has built up inside.

1 The magma chamber fills up.

2 Gases are trapped by the thick magma and build up.

3 Magma flows toward the surface at the weakest point, often the crater or another vent.

4 A bulge may appear on the side of the volcano where the blocked magma is building up.

5 The blockage is released and the sudden pressure causes ash and lava bombs to be thrown out.

6 Thinner lava oozes from the crater or side vent.

7 The column of ash is held by the pressure, and clouds drift over the surrounding area.

8 As the pressure drops, the column collapses and causes a pyroclastic flow, zooming down the sides.

Volcanic Explosivity Index (VEI)

The VEI records and compares eruptions, including how much rock fragments are thrown out, how high the column of ash reaches, and how long the blast lasts. Each number in the index is 10 times more powerful than the last.

PLUME HEIGHT:
2–9 miles (3–15 km)
FRAGMENTS:
353,147,000 cu ft (more than 10,000,000 m³)

PLUME HEIGHT:
328–3,280 ft (100 m–1 km)
FRAGMENTS:
More than 353,100 cu ft (10,000 m³)

PLUME HEIGHT:
½–3 miles (1–3 km)
FRAGMENTS:
33,314,700 cu ft (more than 1,000,000 m³)

PLUME HEIGHT:
6–15½ miles (10–2!
FRAGMENTS:
0.02 cu mile (more than 0.1 km³)

PLUME HEIGHT:
less than 326 ft (100 m)
FRAGMENTS:
Less than 353,100 cu ft (10,000 m³)

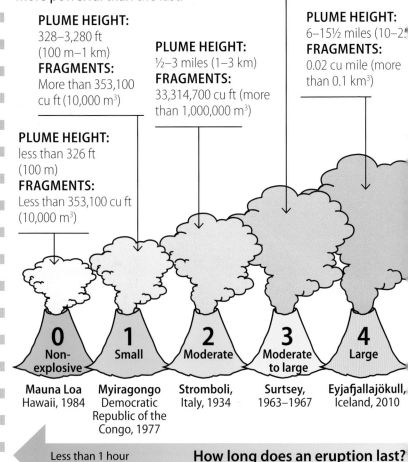

0 Non-explosive
Mauna Loa Hawaii, 1984

1 Small
Myiragongo Democratic Republic of the Congo, 1977

2 Moderate
Stromboli, Italy, 1934

3 Moderate to large
Surtsey, 1963–1967

4 Large
Eyjafjallajökull, Iceland, 2010

Less than 1 hour

How long does an eruption last?

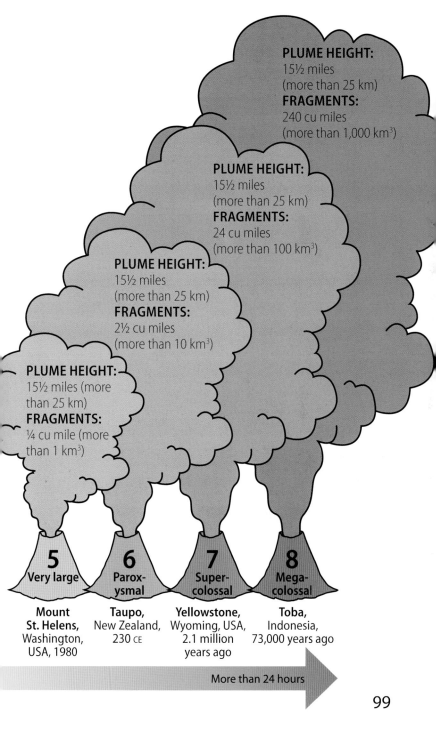

PLUME HEIGHT:
15½ miles
(more than 25 km)
FRAGMENTS:
240 cu miles
(more than 1,000 km³)

PLUME HEIGHT:
15½ miles
(more than 25 km)
FRAGMENTS:
24 cu miles
(more than 100 km³)

PLUME HEIGHT:
15½ miles
(more than 25 km)
FRAGMENTS:
2½ cu miles
(more than 10 km³)

PLUME HEIGHT:
15½ miles (more
than 25 km)
FRAGMENTS:
¼ cu mile (more
than 1 km³)

5
Very large

6
Paroxysmal

7
Super-colossal

8
Mega-colossal

Mount St. Helens,
Washington,
USA, 1980

Taupo,
New Zealand,
230 CE

Yellowstone,
Wyoming, USA,
2.1 million
years ago

Toba,
Indonesia,
73,000 years ago

More than 24 hours

Top 5 Deadliest Eruptions

Throughout history, the unexpected awakening of the sleeping giants have been deadly, and warnings shouldn't be ignored.

NAME Tambora

LOCATION Sumbawa, Indonesia

DATE April 5–12, 1815

DEATHS 92,000–100,000

The roar of the blast was heard more than 800 miles (1,000 km) away. The ash suffocated people and caused winter temperatures in summer around the world.

NAME Unzen

LOCATION Japan

DATE May 21, 1792

DEATHS 14,500–15,000

The lava dome collapsed, causing an avalanche. This also triggered a tsunami, which raced ashore to cause devastation and resulted in most of the deaths.

NAME Krakatoa

LOCATION island of Indonesia

DATE August 26–27, 1883

DEATHS 36,400

In the loudest bang on Earth, the explosion caused the volcano to collapse below sea level. The shock waves in the atmosphere circled Earth at least seven times.

NAME Mount Pelée

LOCATION Martinique

DATE May 8, 1902

DEATHS 30,000–40,000

The massive, hurtling cloud of steam, gas, and ash took two minutes to speed down the mountain and swallow up the city of St. Pierre. Only one person survived.

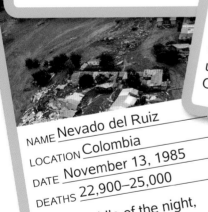

NAME Nevado del Ruiz

LOCATION Colombia

DATE November 13, 1985

DEATHS 22,900–25,000

In the middle of the night, a deadly lahar (volcanic mudslide) swept down the river valleys, burying four towns, including the main city of Armero.

Only about 150 of more than 3,000 volcanoes in the world are being monitored.

Visit the World's Supervolcanoes!

LAKE TOBA

This stunning, city-size crater lake in Indonesia is one of the deepest lakes in the world. It forms the caldera of a supervolcano that last erupted 74,000 years ago, instantly destroying a vast area. Ash fell over South East Asia and the cloud was one of the causes of the Earth's ice ages.

YELLOWSTONE

The 45 mile (72 km) caldera of this supervolcano in Wyoming, USA, stretches the length of the Yellowstone National Park. The last of its three supereruptions was 640,000 years ago, and ash fell across the whole of the USA. The caldera has over 250 geysers actively erupting.

CHAPTER 7
Escaping the Shadow

Carlo couldn't tear his eyes away from the volcano. As more and more ash continued to gush out from the crater, the giant gray cloud grew bigger and bigger. Lightning flickered and flashed across the dark sky. Then Carlo saw something else— what looked like a river of mud and ash racing down the mountain toward them, mowing down all the trees in the way!

He thought of the ancient people of Pompeii and Herculaneum buried

NORMAL   WATCH

beneath the ash from Mt. Vesuvius. Is that what would happen to him if the river of mud and ash caught up with them? He remembered his mother saying these pyroclastic flows could destroy everything in their path.

Pyroclastic Facts

1 Pyroclastic flows are high-speed avalanches of hot ash, rock fragments, and toxic gas.

2 Ignimbrites and nuée ardentes are two types of pyroclastic flows.

3 Ignimbrites contain low-density pumice stones and can travel more than 125 miles (200 km).

4 Nuée ardents contain dense fragments and can travel more than 30 miles (50 km).

5 A flow can move at more than 60 miles (100 km) per hour.

6 The speed depends on the fluidity of the fragments and the steepness of the slope.

7 A flow's temperature can reach over 1,300°F (700°C).

8 Pyroclastic surges move faster and contain lots of gases.

9 Lahars, or volcanic mudflows, are created when water mixes with a pyroclastic flow.

10 Pyroclastic flows and lahars are the most deadly volcanic hazards because of the high temperature and speed.

11 Anything in the flow's path will burn and be destroyed.

12 The most famous pyroclastic flows include Mount Pinatubo, Mount St. Helens, and Mount Pelée.

"Faster, Mama! Faster!" Carlo called out. Rosa didn't take her eyes off the road, but Carlo saw the determined look on her face, and he knew that she was going

NORMAL   WATCH

as fast as she could. He hoped it was fast enough. Carlo kept looking back. It was as if the mud and ash were chasing them!

They were in a race for their lives. Carlo hoped they'd had enough of a headstart. He sat very still in the sidecar, his heart pumping fast. He felt as if he couldn't breathe. Next to him, the mayor's eyes were still squeezed shut. Carlo turned his gaze away from the river of mud and ash and looked straight ahead, toward the glistening bay in the distance.

Still they kept going and going. Carlo ventured another glance behind, afraid he would see that they were about to be swallowed up by the river of mud and ash. What he saw made him smile! The river of mud and ash had slowed down on the flat ground at the foot of the mountain. It wouldn't catch up with them now!

Carlo gave his mom the thumbs-up sign and she smiled. She pointed to what looked like a few big snowflakes, fluttering down from the sky. Carlo thought it was strange to have snow so late in the spring, especially when it wasn't even cold outside. However, when he looked closer, he saw that the snowflakes were black. He suddenly realized that they weren't snowflakes at all, but flakes of ash falling to the ground from the ash cloud. As Carlo watched, what started as a few flakes soon built up to a blizzard of ash, turning the sky black and even covering the countryside in a blanket of black ash.

Through the ash blizzard they could see lights in the distance. As they approached, Rosa started cheering, and soon Carlo, Aldo, and even the mayor all joined in. They had reached the end of the exclusion zone! They were safe at last!

NORMAL   WATCH

Rosa parked the little scooter outside the evacuation center. Paramedics immediately got a stretcher for the mayor and carried him inside. Aldo followed.

Rosa and Carlo sat together in the sidecar. Flakes of ash were still falling around them.

"Well, we made it," said Rosa, giving Carlo an affectionate squeeze. "We're safe and sound."

"Yeah," said Carlo thoughtfully. "It was close, wasn't it? But we actually escaped from the volcano."

Just then, he noticed an orange glow peeking through the ash cloud over the top of Vesuvius. "Is that some hot lava coming out of the volcano now?" he asked.

"No, I think Vesuvius was mostly ash and gas," his mother said. "That's what made such a massive blast."

NORMAL WATCH

"What's that orange light then?" asked Carlo.

As he watched, the orange light grew into a big orange ball. It was the Sun, setting over the mountain. Streaks of orange, pink, and purple filled the sky. The giant gray ash cloud glowed with beautiful colors.

Rosa and Carlo gazed at the sunset in wonder, glad to be together and glad to be alive.

ADVISORY

WARNING

Ring, Ring! Ring, Ring!

Mrs. Carelli *(picking up phone):*
Salve! Hello!

Rosa:
Mama!

Mrs. Carelli:
Rosa, is it you? Thank goodness.
We've been so worried about you. Are
you safe? Are you hurt? Is Carlo alright?

Rosa:
We're both fine although it was
a narrow escape.

Mrs. Carelli:
We saw television pictures of Vesuvius
erupting. The explosion has devastated
the west side. Where were you when
the eruption happened?

Rosa:
We were on the mountain still.
The mayor had refused to leave
Montevista, but then the violent
earthquake happened just before
the main eruption. So Carlo and I
returned to the village piazza to find
him and the TV journalist, who was
with him. Scootering back down the
mountainside was pretty hair-raising.

Mrs. Carelli:
You risked your life for them? You are
crazy! What a relief you are safe!

Rosa:
Everybody is. There are just a handful of people who were hurt in the rush to evacuate and some others who have breathing problems due to the ash falling.

Mrs. Carelli:
Where are you now?

Rosa:
We're at an evacuation center on the outskirts of Naples. Everybody is being looked after well. The emergency services and the local people have provided us with food and bedding.

Mrs. Carelli:
Can I speak to Carlo?

Rosa:
Of course.

Carlo:
Ciao, Nonna! Hello, Grandma!

Mrs. Carelli:
Carlo! Wonderful to hear your voice! I hear you've had quite an adventure, my brave boy.

Carlo:
Yes. It was terrifying at the time, but thrilling thinking back on the eruption, now. Vesuvius certainly woke up from the shadows like a giant. The mountain is still gushing ash. It's an incredible sight.

Mrs. Carelli:
Your grandpa and I are so relieved that you are both safe. . .

Volcano Fact File 4

DATA:
VISCOSITY

The viscosity of a flow means how thick and sticky the lava is. This depends on the amount of silica crystals the different types of lava contain and its temperature. More silica means thicker, stickier lava (and more ★★★).

TYPES OF LAVA FLOWS

* ★ PAHOEHOE LAVA is a thin and fluid, fast-moving lava made from basalt with a smooth rolling surface. As it dries, it turns black and becomes crusty.

* ★ AA LAVA is a basalt-based lava flow with a rough surface made of broken pieces of lava called clinkers. The lava is like a thick, slow-moving paste that buries the clinkers traveling on the top of the flow.

* ★ PILLOW LAVA forms when basalt-based lava flows into the sea, cooling the lava quickly, making a ball or pillow shape. The lava flow forces an opening and forms another pillow shape, and then another and so on.

* ★★ ANDESITIC LAVA is a short-distance viscous flow, containing smooth-sided block-like lava.

* ★★★ DACITIC LAVA is a slow-moving, thick, rounded, and viscous, light gray lava flow with big pockets of gas.

* ★★★ RHYOLITIC LAVA is a thick, very slow-moving lava flow that cools to form a black glassy lava field of glassy obsidian.

Epilogue

The Aldo Rizzo Show

Aldo: *Ciao*, everyone! Today I'm back in Montevista, a very special little village, on the slopes of Mount Vesuvius. It was a year ago today that Mount Vesuvius erupted with a force unknown since the ancient days of Pompeii and Herculaneum. But thanks to some very special people, I am still alive, and I am here today to tell the story. Let me introduce Rosa

Carelli, a volcanologist with the
Vesuvius Observation Center, and
her son, Carlo, who saved my life.

(Applause.)

Mayor: And mine.

Aldo: Yes, and the life of Mayor
Fabiano, too. Thanks to Rosa's
perseverence and courage. . .

Rosa: And Carlo's—

Aldo: Yes, thanks to Rosa *and* Carlo,
everyone in Montevista
evacuated in time.

Mayor: And the only injury was my
sprained ankle. But it could have
been a lot worse. I'm going to
admit it in front of everyone on
TV. I was wrong, and Rosa Carelli
was right.

Rosa: *(laughing)* Why, Mayor Fabiano,
how noble of you to say so.

Mayor: Seriously, Rosa, I was more stubborn than a bull. You and your team of scientists warned us that the volcano would erupt and I ignored you. All I was interested in was the annual village festival—

Aldo: *(interrupts)* Ah yes, the Montevista Festival! This year, amid the ruin caused by the volcano…

(Video footage of the village in ruins after the volcano.)

… the people of Montevista are celebrating their survival. They've been rebuilding their village…

(Camera zooms out to show the village in the middle of being rebuilt. There's a new piazza with buildings under construction around it, and the piazza itself is decorated with stalls and banners for the festival.)

... and they have much to look forward to. So now, without further ado, our guests of honor will officially open this year's Montevista Festival!

(Rosa and Carlo both hold the scissors to cut the official festival ribbon.)

Rosa: Thank you, Aldo. Thank you, Mayor. And thank you to Carlo, my brave son. *(Carlo blushes.)* We hope that Vesuvius won't erupt again for a long, long time, but one never knows...

Carlo: And in the meantime, let's all have plenty of fun!

(Together, Rosa and Carlo cut the ribbon opening the festival.)

Mayor: I now declare the Montevista Festival officially open!

In the Shadow of the Volcano Quiz

See if you can remember the answers to these questions about what you have read.

1. In which country is Mount Vesuvius?

2. What was Rosa Carelli's job?

3. Which two ancient Roman towns were destroyed in the eruption in 79 CE?

4. When was the last violent eruption of Mount Vesuvius?

5. Why did Mayor Fabiano not evacuate Montevista?

6. What does sulfur smell like?

7. Why had a bump formed on the west side of Mount Vesuvius?

8. What sort of sides does a shield volcano have?

9. Where is basalt mostly formed?

10. When was the major eruption of Mount St. Helens?

11. What type of volcano is Kilauea in Hawaii?

12. What happened just before the main eruption blast?

13. Why is a pyroclastic flow deadly?

14. What was the effect of the Tambora volcanic eruption?

15. Name two of the world's supervolcanoes.

Answers on page 125.

Glossary

Aftershocks
Smaller earthquakes that follow a large one.

Evacuation
To move someone away from danger to a safe place.

Exclusion zone
An area that the public is not allowed to enter.

Funicular
A mountainside railway where the tramlike cars are moved along rails by cables.

Harmonic tremor
The continuous rhythms of an earthquake that come just before and during a volcanic eruption.

Infrared
An invisible wave of light that is used in electronic devices to communicate with each other.

Magma
Red-hot liquid rock below the surface of the Earth.

Observation Center
A place where volcanologists monitor a volcano.

Piazza
A square or marketplace in an Italian town.

Pyroclastic flow
High-speed flow of hot ash, rock fragments, and toxic gas.

Richter scale
The scale that measures the magnitude of an earthquake.

Seismic
The vibrations of an earthquake.

Specimen
A sample of something to study or display.

Spectrometer
A device that measures and analyzes the gases in a volcanic plume.

Suffocate
To die from lack of air or being unable to breathe.

Sulfur
A pale yellow chemical, which, when mixed with oxygen (dioxide), becomes a colorless gas with a strong smell.

Thermal
Using, producing, or causing heat.

Tiltmeter
A device that measures the very small changes in the movement of the ground.

VEX
A robotic vehicle called Volcanic Explorer used in high-risk volcanic areas, which transmits data back to an Observation Center.

Volcanologist
A person who studies volcanoes.

Answers to In the Shadow of the Volcano Quiz:
1. Italy; **2.** Volcanologist; **3.** Pompeii and Herculaneum; **4.** 1944;
5. He didn't want to cancel the village festival; **6.** Rotten eggs;
7. Blocked magma was building up; **8.** Low, gently sloping sides;
9. On ocean floors; **10.** 1980; **11.** Shield volcano;
12. An earthquake; **13.** Its high temperature and speed;
14. Caused winter temperatures in summer around the world;
15. Lake Toba and Yellowstone.

Index

active 6, 24, 25, 36, 46, 70
ash 8, 9, 18, 22–23, 38–39, 44, 48, 67, 71, 82, 84, 94, 96, 98, 100, 102–104, 107, 109–111, 113, 115
caldera 39, 102, 103
crater 7, 11, 14, 15, 24–26, 28, 30, 34, 38, 40, 45, 59, 67, 70, 94, 96, 102, 104
dormant 6, 36, 46, 71
earthquake 14, 19, 20–21, 27, 41, 49, 54, 79, 80, 84, 88
evacuation 8, 9, 16, 45, 58, 59
  centers 59, 68, 69, 111, 115
exclusion zone 59, 95, 110
extinct 6, 41
gases 19, 28, 30, 37, 56, 71, 84–85, 96, 107, 117
Herculaneum 18, 62, 104, 118
Kilauea 70
Krakatoa 101
lahars 85, 101, 107
lapilli 82, 83
lava 4, 18, 24–25, 37–39, 44–45, 48, 50, 66, 70, 83, 96, 111, 116–117
  bombs 44, 67, 71, 82, 96
  flow 44, 70, 117
  types 117
magma 6, 7, 17, 28, 29, 50–53, 56, 71, 96
Mauna Loa 54–55, 98
Mount Pelée 101, 107
Mount Pinatubo 55, 107
Mount St. Helens 54–55, 67, 71, 80, 84, 99, 107

Mount Vesuvius 4–5, 12, 22, 24, 26, 55, 59, 65, 79, 105, 118
  79 CE 22
  1944 44–45
  eruptions 24–25
Nevado del Ruiz 101
Observation Center 4, 18, 21, 26, 28, 30, 33, 34, 73, 119
Pompeii 18, 22–23, 62, 104, 108
pumice 83
pyroclastic flow 18, 71, 95–96, 105, 107
Ring of Fire 54
rocks 19, 22, 28, 40–43, 46, 48–50, 71, 79, 83–85, 98, 107
  basalt 42, 50, 117
  crystals 47, 51
  gabbro 47, 51
  granite 47, 51
  obsidian 50, 117
  pegmatite 51
  samples 27, 37
spectrometer 37
sulfur 22, 27, 28, 91
Tambora 55, 100
tiltmeters 28–29
Toba 99, 102
Unzen 100
vent 7, 38, 39, 96
VEX 27, 29–31, 35
volcanic explosivity index 98
volcanologist 11, 15, 36, 37, 52, 66, 70, 85, 119
Yellowstone 99, 103

About the Author

Caryn Jenner writes and edits a variety of books for children of all ages, including both fiction and non-fiction. For DK Publishing, she has written *Eyewitness Workbook: Earth*, as well as several titles in the *DK Readers* series. Her picture book, *Starting School*, was one of the eight books longlisted for the UK's 2012 School Library Association Information Book Award in the Under 7s age group.

Caryn also teaches English to speakers of other languages and volunteers at a local school. She grew up in the USA, but has made her home in the UK for many years. She lives in London with her husband, daughter, and three cats.

About the Consultant

Dr. Linda Gambrell, Distinguished Professor of Education at Clemson University, has served as President of the National Reading Conference, the College Reading Association, and the International Reading Association. She is also reading consultant to the *DK Readers*.

Here are some other
DK Adventures you might enjoy.

Terrors of the Deep
Marine biologists Dom and Jake take their deep-sea
submersible down into the world's deepest, darkest
ocean trench, the Mariana Trench.

Horse Club
Emma is so excited—she is going to
horseback-riding camp with her older sister!

Clash of the Gladiators
Travel back in time to ancient Rome, when gladiators
entertained the crowds. Will they be spared death?

The Mummy's Curse
Are our intrepid time travelers cursed? Experience ancient
Egyptian life along the banks of the Nile with them.

Ballet Academy
Lucy follows her dream as she trains to be a professional
dancer at the Academy. Will she make it through?

Galactic Mission
Year 2098: planet Earth is dying. Five schoolchildren
embark on a life or death mission to the distant star system
of Alpha Centauri to find a new home.

Twister: A Terrifying Tale of Superstorms
Jeremy joins his cousins in Tornado Alley for the vacation.
To his surprise, he discovers they are storm chasers and
has the ride of his life!